What Happens to Baby Teeth?

A tooth Fairy Story.

Written and Illustrated by
Marvin Tweedy

1

Dedicated to Jordan, Zachary, Grant, Alex, Bella, and Paisley my grandkids!!

Bag of Teeth

Have you ever wondered what the tooth fairy does with all those baby teeth that kids lose and put under their pillows?

Me Too! So, I set out to find what happens to those teeth.

It seemed like the only way I could figure this out was to actually catch the tooth fairy. I knew I would somehow have to capture the tooth fairy and make her take me with her. After all, I cannot fly and the tooth fairy makes it all around the world each night. So she must fly to be able to go that far.

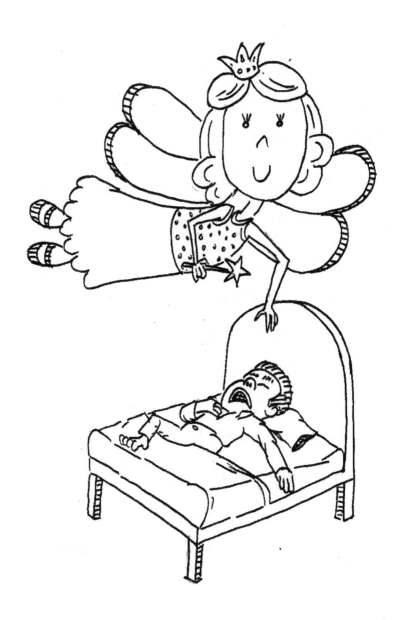

To catch a tooth fairy, I decided I needed bait. The only bait I could think of was my baby tooth. It took until my ninth birthday when I finally lost another baby tooth. I thought about hiding it someplace where she would not find it; like in my underwear. But I could not go to sleep with the tooth in my underwear, so I just held it in my hand.

After halfway through the night, I was sleeping well. But I WOKE UP when the tooth fairy tried to get the tooth out of my hand! I told her, "You cannot have my tooth unless you take me with

you and show me what you do with baby teeth!" She very quickly told me, "NO, NO, NO you can't go because I have too much distance to cover in one night." I pleaded with her to just tell me what she does with all those teeth! She refused but said she would tell me if I guessed right.

All I could imagine was putting them in a sort of tooth junk yard. Yuck! All those stinky rotting baby teeth just smelling in the hot sun. I told her what I was thinking.

"No, that is not it," she said as she grabbed my tooth and jumped

right out the window before I could even move!

I had to wait almost six more months to lose another baby tooth, but with a lot of wiggling and pulling I finally managed to get one out.

Again, I was determined to catch the tooth fairy. During the six months I waited, I decided that she must grind the teeth up and made fairy dust for flying out of them. But I had to get her to admit it.

This time I put my tooth inside a small match box and put the box inside a small jar. Then! I put the

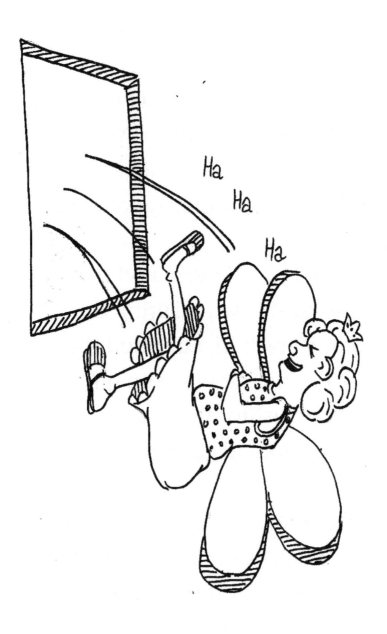

jar under my pillow. No way was she going to get away this time.

Well, it worked! I woke up as she tried to slip the jar out; before she even got to the box. I grabbed her wrist and said, "You cannot go until you tell me what you do with baby teeth." She finally agreed to tell me like before but, only if I guessed right.

I took a big long breath and talking as fast as I could, I explained that she takes all the teeth and grinds them up to make fairy dust for flying. I just knew I was right.

You know what? She started laughing so hard that she fell right out the window. No doubt I was wrong to get her to laugh that hard.

I had to go back to the drawing board, if I was going to figure this out. I researched all about tooth fairies. I found that some people think the tooth fairy is making a big fairy castle out of all those teeth. That had to be it. I started wiggling my teeth again. It seemed that I would never lose another tooth.

Well, I was almost 11 when I finally lost my next tooth despite all the wiggling.

To hide my tooth this time... I thought and thought. Then I remembered that I got a new toy for Christmas. It was an army soldier with a built-in motion sensor. That motion senor would work to protect my tooth.

I locked my baby tooth in a box with a padlock and put the box where the solder's sensor would be activated!

This time I woke up just as she was going out my window. I grabbed her ankle and said, "I will

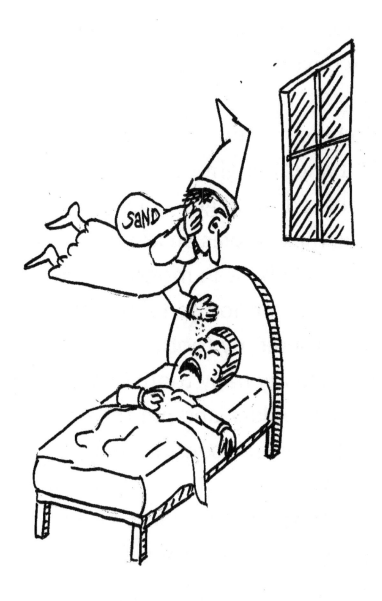

not let you go unless you tell me what you do with all those baby teeth." Again, she agreed to tell me the truth but only if I guessed right. As before, I took a deep breath and started talking as fast as I could. I said, "I know you are using them to make a great big beautiful fairy castle for you to live in." She replied very quickly, "No" and jumped out the window before I could get another guess in.

I went back to thinking, wiggling teeth and making guesses at what happens to baby teeth. One day my uncle told me a story about the Sandman. My uncle

said, "The Sandman puts you to sleep by putting sand in your eyes. That is why you have grit in the corners of your eyes when you wake up."

Maybe that is what the tooth fairy does. Perhaps she is working with the sandman and gives him the ground up teeth to use as sand to put in people's eyes when they wake up. They are in cahoots with each other! That is why they cannot talk about it.

Mom told me that I was almost out of baby teeth. I had only one baby tooth left. Then I would not have any more teeth fall

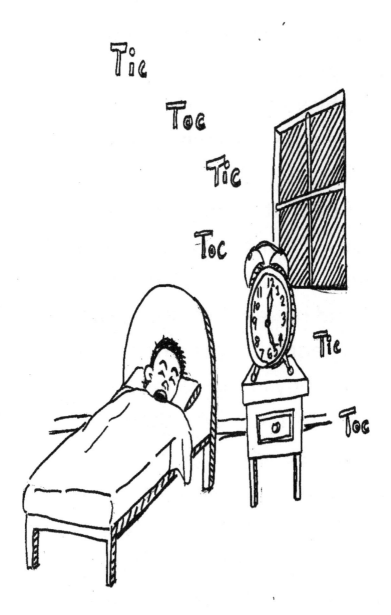

out until I lost my wisdom teeth when I was an adult.

I had just one more shot to get this figured out! I had to get ready. I nailed all the windows shut. I locked the door. I put my motion sensor soldier out. I put my last baby tooth in a box, put the box in a jar and put the jar under my pillow. No tooth fairy was ever going to get into my room let alone get out with my last baby tooth!

I was ready and I was going to stay up all night if necessary. I looked at my clock and it was 11:00 pm. I looked again later, and it was 2:00 am. Suddenly, I looked again and it was 7:00 am. I had fallen asleep!

No way the tooth fairy could have gotten my very last baby tooth. I scrambled out of bed and looked. It was gone!!! Somehow, after three times of catching her, I had missed her.

I will never know what she does with all those baby teeth unless when I lose my wisdom teeth, I can catch her.

Hmmmmmm.

Look out tooth fairy. I am
going to figure this out....

Just not today.

Printed in Great Britain
by Amazon